THE DINOSAUR THAT POOPED CHRISTMAS

For Dougie, From Tom

For Tom, From Dougie

THE DINOSAUR THAT POOPED CHRISTMAS
A RED FOX BOOK 978 1 849 41779 2

Published in Great Britain by Red Fox,

an imprint of Random House Children's Publishers UK
A Random House Group Company

This edition published 2012

1 3 5 7 9 10 8 6 4 2

Red Fox Books are published by Random House Children's Publishers UK,
61–63 Uxbridge Road, London W5 5SA

www.kidsatrandomhouse.co.uk
www.totallyrandombooks.co.uk
www.randomhouse.co.uk

Addresses for companies within The Random House Group Limited
can be found at: www.randomhouse.co.uk/offices.htm

THE RANDOM HOUSE GROUP Limited Reg. No. 954009

A CIP catalogue record for this book is available from the British Library.

Printed in Italy

The Random House Group Limited supports the Forest Stewardship Council (FSC®), the leading international
forest certification organization. Our books carrying the FSC label are printed on FSC®-certified paper. FSC is
the only forest certification scheme endorsed by the leading environmental organizations, including Greenpeace.
Our paper procurement policy can be found at www.randomhouse.co.uk/environment.

THE DINOSAUR THAT POOPED CHRISTMAS

Tom Fletcher and Dougie Poynter
Illustrated by Garry Parsons

RED FOX

From high in the sky Santa looked down below
To houses all cosy and covered in snow.
Where snoozers were snoozing, tucked up in their beds
Whilst dreaming the most festive dreams in their heads.

But one boy called Danny, a greedy young chap,
The greediest chap on the planet in fact,
Was lying awake on his mountain of toys,
Which stood even taller than most girls and boys.

But that wasn't enough, Danny still wanted more,
He wanted much more than his toy box could store.

So big Santy C said, "I'll leave him a present,
But this year his present might just be unpleasant."

Danny heard
such a clatter,
his heart skipped
a thump –
'Twas the clopping
of hooves going
clippety-clump.

He bounced out of bed and threw on some clothes

And crept
down the stairs
on his tip-tippy-toes.

There, under the tree, were gifts big and small
And a

GIMUNGUS

egg placed in front of them all.

"An egg?!" Danny said. "Santa brought me an egg?!"

Then out with a

crack!
popped a dinosaur's head!

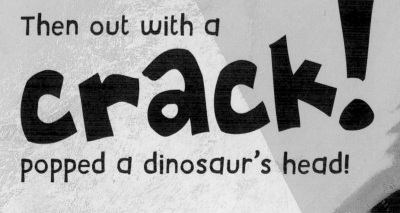

It wasted no time on that cold Christmas morning
And started to eat everything without warning.

It swallowed the stockings and Christmas cards too,
The red fairy lights, then the green and the blue.
There wasn't a single thing Danny could do,
Except sit and watch as the dinosaur chewed.

It chewed and it munched and it crunched on Kris Kringle,
The reindeer, the sleigh bells and all things that jingle.

But it didn't stop there, there were more things to gobble,
Much more than the small shiny baubles that bobble.

It ate up the cat and the dog and the fish,
And from the dishwasher it downed every dish.
The tables, the chairs, the walls and the doors –
Now nothing was safe, not even the floors.

Now, reader
BEWARE,
the next part is scary,
And if you read on
you'll need new underweary.

Danny's poor granny was knitting some socks,
But the dino had no need for socks, it had lots!

So it slurped up her knitting like strings of spaghetti
And gobbled up Granny along with the settee.

Then it ate Danny's mum,
she was gone in one bite,
And although Danny's dad
tried to put up a fight,

The dino had grown to
the size of King Kong.
With a gulp and a burp
Danny's father was gone.

Now nothing was left –
all Danny could see
Was a fat dinosaur
where his home used to be.

And so, with the thought
of no Christmas this year,
His tears turned to snowflakes
and then disappeared.

With the feeling of guilt
in the dinosaur's gut,

Its brain brewed a plan
involving its butt.

It knew there was only one thing it could do:
To put Christmas right it needed to . . .

It pooped out the turkey, the toys and the telly,
And even the tinsel was now brown and smelly.
It pooped all the presents and pieces of puzzles,
It pooped all the things it had previously guzzled.
And then Father Christmas yelled "OUT OF THE WAY!"
As he flew from the dinosaur's bum on his sleigh.

The dinosaur finally gave a huge push
And pooped Danny's parents in one massive

whoooOOOSH!

Last, but not least,
and never forgotten,
Granny plopped out
of the dinosaur's bottom.

"Merry Christmas," said Dan to his whole family
As they washed off the presents and put up the tree.
And the greedy young chap that you saw just before
Promised next Christmas he'd not ask for more.

And the dinosaur
promised he'd
not eat a crumb . . .

. . . as you would if Christmas came out of your bum!